Betty and the YETI

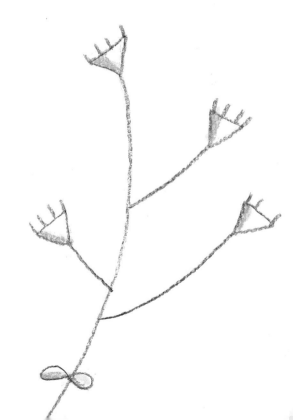

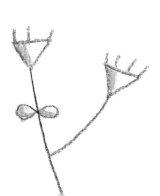

Ella Burfoot

Macmillan Children's Books

Betty has a little red sled
that she takes wherever she goes.

For Lila and Cyril

First published 2010 by Macmillan Children's Books
This edition published 2011 by Macmillan Children's Books
a division of Macmillan Publishers Limited
20 New Wharf Road, London N1 9RR
Basingstoke and Oxford
Associated companies throughout the world
www.panmacmillan.com

ISBN: 978-1-4472-0267-7

Text and illustrations copyright © Ella Burfoot 2010
Moral rights asserted.

3 5 7 9 8 6 4 2

A CIP catalogue record for this book is
available from the British Library.

Printed in China

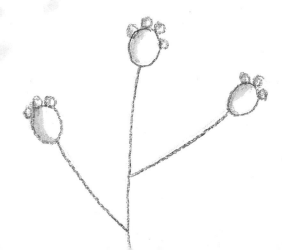

She pulls on the ropes
and flies down the slopes,
whether it freezes or snows.

Betty finds things in the snow
when she goes out to play.
She puts them gently on her sled
and then goes on her way.

One day she found a pair of gloves
— she put them on her sled,

and a jingly jangly fluffy hat,
which she wore upon her head.

And when she saw some snow boots,
as hairy as a bear,
she tried them on her little feet
and stamped from here to there.

Then she found a woolly scarf,
all thick with twigs and leaves,

and one enormous smelly coat
that came right past her knees.

"Do these clothes belong to you?"
Betty asked a polar bear.
"No," he said, and shook his head,
"I don't need clothes to wear.

"I've got thick fur to keep me warm,
I do not mean to gloat.
But I've no need for hats or scarves
and never wear a coat."

"Do these clothes belong to you?"
Betty asked a big blue whale.
"No," Whale said, and shook her head,
and splashed her great big tail.

"I've got blubber to keep me warm,
— a special kind of fat.
Though I *do* like the bells
on that jingly jangly hat."

"Do these clothes belong to *you*?"
Betty asked an arctic hare.
"No," he said, and shook his head,
"ask that rock over there."

What a strange thing, thought Betty,
peering at the rock.
But I've asked a hare and a polar bear,
so I can't see why not!

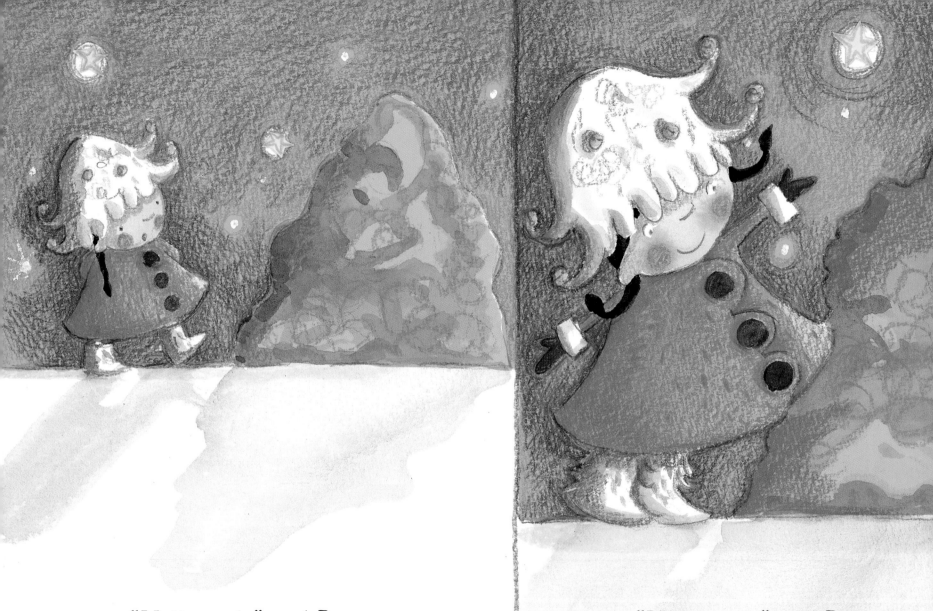

"Hello rock," said Betty.
The rock did not reply.

"Hello rock," said Betty.
The rock was very shy.

But finally there came a voice
that said to little Betty,

"I'm really not a rock at all,
I'm actually a . . .

. . . Yeti!"

"A yeti!" squealed Betty,
and she tried to run away.
But, "Please don't go!" the yeti cried,
"I'd love it if you'd stay."

"Yetis in the wild, you see,
are rather shy and small.
We have to wear a lot of clothes
to keep us warm at all.

"My clothes are big and hairy
— they give folk such a shock
that I threw them all away
and hid behind this rock.

"It's very hard to make a friend
in the land of snow
when you've scared them all away
before you've even said 'hello!'"

Betty didn't fret at all
— she handed him his clothes.
"You'd better put these on," she said,
"before it really snows."

She took his muddy glove
in her little mittened hand,
and talked with him and walked with him
across the frozen land.

Soon they met Betty's friends
in the cold and snowy night.
And the smelly hairy yeti?
Well, he gave them quite a fright!

But when they saw that Betty
had hold of Yeti's paw,
they knew they didn't need to be
frightened any more.

And the hare spoke up quite bravely
in a loud and cheerful voice,
"I'd befriend a yeti,
given half a choice!"

So Whale and Bear and Arctic Hare
became the yeti's friends.
The yeti kept his clothes on
and was never cold again.

Betty made a hat like his
— she wore it every day.
And when she went out on her sled,
she jingled all the way!

You won't often see a Yeti
in the land of ice and snow,
because unless they've
met you once or twice
they're still quite
shy you know!
Betty
x